Good Neighbors

Diane Redfield Massie

AEP

AMERICAN EDUCATION PUBLICATIONS / A XEROX COMPANY

Middletown, Connecticut

Copyright © 1972 by Diane Redfield Massie

Publishing, Executive, and Editorial Offices:
American Education Publications,
245 Long Hill Road
Middletown, Connecticut 06457
Subscription Offices:
Educational Center, Columbus, Ohio 43216

Library of Congress Catalog Card Number: 70–186621

Weekly Reader Children's Book Club Edition
Primary Division

for Zoe

Mouse was a pocket mouse. He lived in a cozy little room underground.

"I love my house," said Mouse. "Home sweet home!"

He ran up his tunnel and out into the moonlight.
The desert was silver and still.

"OUCH!" said a voice behind him. "OH, OUCH! again!"
The cactus flowers shook on the cactus plant.

" I'M GETTING IT! OUCH!"

"Who's there?" whispered Mouse. He stood near his tunnel,
ready to run inside.

"I'VE GOT IT!" said the voice.
"Oh, my poor paws!"
A large flower fell down and rolled over.
"Oooooooooh!" said packrat,
coming out. He was wringing
his paws and crying.

"What's the matter?" asked Mouse.

"I've got prickers!" said the packrat. He collected some cactus leaves and dragged them over the sand.

"What are you doing?" asked Mouse, picking up the flower.

"I'm fixing up my doorway," said the packrat, flinging his cactus onto a heap very near Mouse's side yard. "Call me 'Ratty.' We're neighbors."

"We are?" said Mouse.

"I just moved in," said Ratty. "This pile of junk is my front door."

"Really?" said Mouse, moving nearer.

"You can't see my door," said Ratty. "It's underneath there somewhere."

"How do you get in?" asked Mouse.

"It's not easy," said Ratty.

Mouse stared at the heap of sticks and cactus.
Rocks were sprinkled on top. It looked rather like
the dump at the end of town.

Mouse glanced at his own neat doorway,
swept clean that morning. His doorknocker
shone in the moonlight and his door was cactus
green.

"When I'm coming home with groceries,"
said Ratty, picking up a stone, "that's when
there's trouble." He threw the stone at his pile
and smacked his paws. "Things have a way of getting
caught. You know how it is with prickers. The bags rip
and there you have it—a mess!"

"Why do you cover up your door that way?" asked Mouse, sitting down on his step.

"Camouflage," said Ratty. "If you throw a pile of junk in front of your house, nobody knows you *live* there."

"Don't you *want* anyone to know?" asked Mouse, smelling his flower.

Ratty straightened a stick on top of his pile
and stepped back. "Not bad! It's even worse
looking than my other house! I had to move because
of badgers," said Ratty, poking his nose between the sticks
and cactus leaves. He pushed his way down and disappeared
beneath. "OUCH!" said Ratty, looking out again. "Like
to come inside for a spot of tea?"

"Well," said Mouse, staring at the cactus
prickers, "I think I'd better go home.
It's my suppertime, you see, and . . ."
"Tomorrow then," said Ratty, waving
his paw. "See you tomorrow, Neighbor! Oh, OUCH!"
and he disappeared again.

Mouse stood for a moment staring
at Ratty's heap at the end of his yard.
The moonlight silvered the cactus
and stones and even the sticks alike.

"But in the morning," said Mouse to
himself, "it will look just like the dump!"
He shook his head and went inside,
shutting his door behind him.

Mouse was up early the next morning,
making his breakfast. His tea-kettle
whistled softly on the stove.

THUMP! THUMP! THUMP!
"What's *that*?" said Mouse, dropping his cup.
Rocks and dirt showered down on his sofa. He
scrambled behind the stove.

"Anybody home?" Ratty
poked his head through a large
hole in Mouse's wall. He pushed
himself through and hopped down
onto the sofa below.

"Bullseye!" said Ratty. "What luck!
I was making my back room a bit longer,
and here it's come into *your* house!"
"So it has!" said Mouse, picking up his cup.
The handle had broken off, which made
him feel even crosser. "Ratty!" he said,
"You've made a large hole in my wall!"

"Isn't that *nice*?" said Ratty, sitting down at
Mouse's breakfast table. "Now we can *really* be
good neighbors! If I need to borrow something,
I can pop right in and out again. You can do
the same, of course. What's mine is yours and what's
yours in mine!"

"What's mine is *not* yours!" said Mouse crossly.
"This is my house and I don't want a hole in my wall!"

"But it's above the sofa," said Ratty,
pouring himself a cup of tea. "It's so handy.
We can just jump down and go, 'Ooooooooooph!' "

"We will not go, 'Ooooooooooph' on anything!"
said Mouse, "and certainly not on *my* sofa!"
He brushed the rocks and dirt off with his paws
and stood up.

The tunnel above ran back to a room where
Ratty's lamp shone faintly.

"This is good tea," said Ratty. "Have you got
any biscuits?"

"No!" said Mouse, jumping down. "I haven't!"

"Do you have any jam?"

"NO!" shouted Mouse. He pounded his fist
on the table, making the teacup jump. The tea
ran down his tablecloth.

"My goodness!" said Ratty. "Why are you so cross?"
He stood up and stretched and then hopped to
the sofa and from there to the hole above.

"See you later!" he said. "Have a little
finishing to do here and there before lunch."

Mouse watched him
disappear up the tunnel.
Then he hurried across the
room to his cupboard
and took down a large,
round picture hanging above.
　"Grandfather Pocket Mouse
will have to cover the hole,"
said Mouse, "until I can patch it up."

He climbed the sofa
and hung the portrait
over a root.
　"There! Who would know
there's a hole at all!"
he said, stepping backward,
and fell off. "DRAT THAT
PACKRAT!" said Mouse,
flinging down a stone.
"GOOD NEIGHBORS! HA!"

By lunchtime, Mouse had cleared
away the stones and dirt from his room.
Then he warmed his tea and ate some toast.
At last he settled down for his morning
nap.

Knock! Knock! Knock!
"What?" said Mouse, rubbing his eyes. "Who's there?"
"ME AGAIN!" said Ratty, pushing out from under
the picture. "I forgot to borrow some cheese."
"CHEESE?" said Mouse.
"And bread," said Ratty, "for lunch."
"LUNCH?" said Mouse.

Ratty jumped down on the sofa. Dust covered
his head and a cactus leaf hung from his ear.

"I said to myself, I said," said Ratty,
" 'Why don't you run down to see your good neighbor, Mouse.
Perhaps you and he can have a little bite to eat
together, being such good neighbors and all.' "
"I've just eaten," said Mouse.
"Anything left?" asked Ratty.

"Ratty," said Mouse sternly, "I think there
are some things you should know. Being good
neighbors means you don't *bother* somebody else!"

"Bother?" said Ratty.

"You don't make holes in somebody's wall! And
you don't borrow cheese and bread and wake
somebody up from his nap!"

"Whose nap?" asked Ratty.

"MY nap!" said Mouse. "You're not being a very
good neighbor, and I'm getting very tired!"

"Why don't you take a nap?"
asked Ratty.

"I'M TRYING TO!"
shouted Mouse.

"I think I'll go home,"
said Ratty. He looked as if
he might cry.
"GOOD-BY!" said Mouse.

Ratty climbed through the hole above
the sofa. The picture swung back
and forth behind him.
"And I hope," said Mouse, pulling up
his covers, "that that's *that*!" He
slept peacefully for the rest of the day.

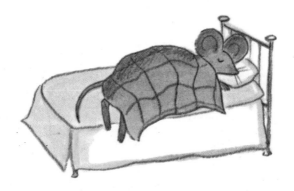

By late afternoon the sun had gone
down and the desert above had grown cooler.
Mouse made his way up his tunnel and ran
out into the moonlight. He gathered
seeds under a bush and found some cactus
apples. "Delicious!" said Mouse, biting
between the prickers. "What a lovely night!
I wonder where everyone is?"

"Watch out!" said a tiny moth. "The badger is out looking for his supper."

"The badger?" said Mouse. "Who's he?"

"The badger is very large," said the moth. "He likes to eat mice and rats."

"Pocket mice?" said Mouse, dropping his seeds.

"Especially pocket mice," said the moth, shutting his wings.

"I think I'll go home," said Mouse. "I think I'll go home right away!"

He ran quickly over the sand, forgetting his apples and seeds.

"There's my house," said Mouse. "Thank Heavens!"
The creosote bushes rustled. Something large was behind them.

"It's the badger!" said Mouse, jumping in the air.
"It's the badger for sure!" He leaped for his door
and shut it behind him.

The badger crept out in the moonlight. He stood
before Mouse's green door.

"Oh, help! help! help!"
cried Mouse, running
about his room.
"I forgot to fasten the
lock!" He hid underneath
his sofa.

THUMP! THUMP! THUMP! The badger
knocked at his door.
    "Help!" said Mouse. "He'll open it! OH, HELP, RATTY!
HELP ME!"

        Ratty looked out from under the picture.
"Give me your paw!" he said. Mouse
reached up and Ratty pulled. Up he went
under the picture into the hole, *and just in time!*

The badger's paw reached down and felt
about the room. His claws tapped the sofa,
the table and chairs, and then he picked up the
stove. "OUCH!" said the Badger, dropping the stove.
"Something's hot in there!" He licked his paw and
shook his fur, and then shuffled off across the sand.

Mouse lay exhausted in Ratty's chair.

"I've made some tea," said Ratty. He
poured Mouse a cup and sat down in his
rocker beside the table.

"Ratty," said Mouse.

"Don't try to talk," said Ratty. "You've had
quite a fright. Just drink your tea and
rest a bit. Would you like a cracker?"

"Ratty," said Mouse. "You saved me . . ."

"Think nothing of it," said Ratty, taking
out his cracker box. "Tomorrow we'll fix
up your room. And I was thinking," said
Ratty, pouring himself some tea, "that
you're quite right about that hole in your wall.
I'll help you patch it up."

"Oh, NO!" said Mouse, dropping his cracker.
"I *like* a hole in my wall. It's so handy
for popping in and out of! We can even go, 'Ooooooooooph!'
on my sofa!"

"We *can?*" said Ratty. "But you said . . ."

"Never mind what I said," said Mouse, "and I don't care if your front door *does* look like the dump!"

"It's so badgers won't know that I live here."

"It's a very good idea," said Mouse. He settled back in Ratty's chair and sipped his cup of tea. "Just a minute!" he said, jumping up again. He ran down the tunnel to his room and disappeared. In a moment he was back, swinging a bag behind him. "I've brought some cheese!" said Mouse.

"HOORAY!" cried Ratty, clapping his paws. "We'll have a supper party!"

"We'll celebrate being neighbors!" said Mouse. "Good neighbors, I mean."

"HOORAY FOR GOOD NEIGHBORS!" cried Ratty, hopping over his chair. He spread out his crackers and smiled at Mouse. "Please pass the cheese."